WS

352

Popp

GRINDLEY, S.

Poppy and Max and too many muffins

70003213999   Pbk

Please return/renew this item by the last date shown

worcestershire
countycouncil
Cultural Services

D0299981

For Jane
SG

For Natalie, a girl who likes her muffins!
LG

Reading Consultant: Prue Goodwin,
lecturer in education at the University of Reading

ORCHARD BOOKS
338 Euston Road, London NW1 3BH
Orchard Books Australia
Hachette Children's Books
Level 17/207 Kent Street, Sydney, NSW 2000
ISBN: 978 1 84362 408 0 (hardback)
ISBN: 978 1 84362 410 3 (paperback)
First published in hardback in Great Britain in 2007
First paperback publication in 2008
Poppy and Max characters © Lindsey Gardiner 2001
Text © Sally Grindley 2007
Illustrations © Lindsey Gardiner 2007

The rights of Sally Grindley to be identified as the author and
of Lindsey Gardiner to be identified as the illustrator of this work
have been asserted by them in accordance with the
Copyright, Designs and Patents Act, 1988.
A CIP catalogue record for this book is available from the British Library.

1 3 5 7 9 10 8 6 4 2 (hardback)
1 3 5 7 9 10 8 6 4 2 (paperback)
Printed in Hong Kong
Orchard Books is a division of Hachette Children's Books,
an Hachette Livre UK company.
www.orchardbooks.co.uk

Poppy and Max and Too Many Muffins

Sally Grindley 🦴 Lindsey Gardiner

ORCHARD BOOKS

WORCESTERSHIRE COUNTY COUNCIL	
999	
Bertrams	18.04.08
	£4.99
WS	

One Sunday afternoon, Poppy and Max were sitting in the garden when Poppy said, "Max, you are putting on weight. You need to do some exercise."

"I am not a dog who does exercise,"
said Max huffily.
"You'll have to stop eating muffins
then," said Poppy.

"What, no muffins?" wailed Max.
"But I love muffins."
He jumped up from his chair and ran
to a tree and back.

"You only ran a few steps,"
Poppy chuckled. "You need to run
a few miles!"
"Bah!" grumbled Max.

"Let's make a plan and do exercises together," said Poppy.
"If we must," grunted Max.

"On Monday let's go for a run in the park," said Poppy.

MONDAY

SWIM

TUESDAY

"On Tuesday let's rest," said Max.
"On Tuesday let's go for a swim," said
Poppy. "And on Wednesday we'll ride
our bikes."

"We should rest on Thursday," said Max.
"On Thursday let's go to the gym," said Poppy. "And on Friday you can come to my dance class with me."

"I am not a dog who goes to dance classes," protested Max. "On Friday I'm resting."

"On Saturday and Sunday we'll rest, and we'll deserve our muffins and hot chocolate," said Poppy.

"What, no muffins except on Saturdays and Sundays?" howled Max. "Too many muffins means too much Max," chuckled Poppy, tickling him.

15

"Bah," grumbled Max. Then
he cheered up. "At least it's
Sunday today!"

The next day, Poppy rose bright
and early.

"Time for our run, Max," she said.

"Bah!" grumbled Max. He grumbled all the way round the park and back again.

On Tuesday he sat shivering on the side of the pool and grumbled about the water being too wet.

On Wednesday he fell off his bike and grumbled about his bruises.

On Thursday he grumbled when a weight fell on his paw.

On Friday he said, "I am not a dog who goes to dance classes, and I am not going now."

"Please come with me," said Poppy. "I'll come with you," said Max, "but I won't dance."

The dance teacher was delighted to see
Max. "Ah," she said, "a podgy doggy.
We'll soon get rid of that tummy."

Max sat down quickly on a bench.
"Leave my tummy alone," he growled.

The music began and Poppy stepped
on to the dance floor.
"Look at me!" Poppy cried as she
twirled round and round.

Max began to tap his feet to the music.
"This is such fun," giggled Poppy.
Max began to sway from side to side.

"Come on, Max, you'll enjoy it,"
laughed Poppy.
Max jumped up and began to twist
and shake and skip and twirl and
twist and shake some more.

Poppy clapped her hands. "Brilliant,
Max!" she cried.
"I'm a great dancer!" Max replied.

When the music stopped at last,
Max flopped down on the bench.
"Phew!" he puffed. "Exercise is
very tiring!"

"Never mind, Max," smiled Poppy.
"It's a rest day tomorrow."
"Never mind rest," said Max gleefully.
"It's a muffin day tomorrow!"

Sally Grindley
Illustrated by Lindsey Gardiner

Poppy and Max and the Lost Puppy	978 1 84362 394 6	£4.99
Poppy and Max and the Snow Dog	978 1 84362 404 2	£4.99
Poppy and Max and the Fashion Show	978 1 84362 393 9	£4.99
Poppy and Max and the Sore Paw	978 1 84362 405 9	£4.99
Poppy and Max and the River Picnic	978 1 84362 395 3	£4.99
Poppy and Max and the Noisy Night	978 1 84362 409 7	£4.99
Poppy and Max and the Big Wave	978 1 84362 519 3	£4.99
Poppy and Max and Too Many Muffins	978 1 84362 410 3	£4.99

Poppy and Max are available from all good bookshops,
or can be ordered direct from the publisher:
Orchard Books, PO BOX 29, Douglas IM99 1BQ
Credit card orders please telephone 01624 836000 or fax 01624 837033
or e-mail: bookshop@enterprise.net for details.

To order please quote title, author and ISBN and your full name and address.
Cheques and postal orders should be made payable to 'Bookpost plc'.
Postage and packing is FREE within the UK
(overseas customers should add £1.00 per book).

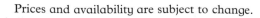

Prices and availability are subject to change.